This Is Ruby

Words by Sara O'Leary

Pictures by Alea Marley

tundra

This is Ruby.

She's so glad to see you.
She can't wait to share her day with you.

Would you like to see her room?

Hello hello!

Ta-da!

And, look, she built herself a little town.

Ruby is always busy.
There are so many things she
wants to do and make and be.

TO do!
INVent
ExPLORe
make Potion

This is Ruby's best friend. His name is Teddy.

Ruby might be an animal conservationist
when she grows up.

Or an astronaut.

Or an engineer.

She hasn't decided yet.
Have you?

Ruby likes to make things.

She likes to watch things grow.

And she likes to figure out how things work.

Ruby knows that there is always
another way to see the world . . .

Ruby and Teddy like to do excavations.
(Her parents call it digging holes.)

Ruby could grow up to be an archaeologist.

Or she might be a doctor one day.

Ruby thinks it's funny that some
people are scared of skeletons.

Everybody has one.
Can you feel yours underneath your skin?

Ruby's created a potion that tastes like clouds.
And she's made a book that has smells
instead of words so animals can read it.

Ruby might be an inventor.

She even invented a time machine.

If you could travel anywhere in time,
where would you go?

Ruby decides to go back to see what
the dinosaurs really looked like.

And then she goes way, way back
to see the day her parents met.

After that, she visits the future.

And then she travels to an
ordinary afternoon from last week.

It was so perfect that she wanted to live it twice.

Ruby's days are very full because she
is curious about so many things.

What kind of things are
you curious about?

Ruby knows that there is no end of things to do,
that she will always find something new to make,
and that she can be whatever she wants to be.

She's looking forward to tomorrow
but her favorite day is today.

She's so glad you were here to share it with her.

For three brilliant girls —
Moira, Fionnuala and Oonagh
— S.O'L.

For Lewis,
my favorite person
— A.M.

Tundra Books, an imprint of Penguin Random House Canada Young Readers,
a division of Penguin Random House of Canada Limited

Library and Archives Canada Cataloguing in Publication

Title: This is Ruby / words by Sara O'Leary ; pictures by Alea Marley.
Names: O'Leary, Sara, author. | Marley, Alea, illustrator.
Identifiers: Canadiana (print) 20200187198 | Canadiana (ebook) 20200187201 | ISBN 9780735263611
   (hardcover) | ISBN 9780735263628 (EPUB)
Classification: LCC PS8579.L293 T45 2021 | DDC jC813/.54—dc23

Published simultaneously in the United States of America by Tundra Books of Northern New York, an imprint of Penguin Random House Canada Young Readers, a division of Penguin Random House of Canada Limited

Library of Congress Control Number: 2020933264

Edited by Tara Walker with assistance from Margot Blankier
Designed by Kelly Hill
The artwork in this book came to be after plenty
   of daydreaming, gazing at old photographs
   and eventually opening Photoshop.
The text was set in Van Dijck.

Printed and bound in China

www.penguinrandomhouse.ca

1 2 3 4 5   25 24 23 22 21

Penguin
Random House
tundra | TUNDRA BOOKS